James Alfred Wanklyn

Tea, Coffee and Cocoa

a practical treatise on the analysis of tea, coffee, cocoa, chocolate, maté

etc.

James Alfred Wanklyn

Tea, Coffee and Cocoa

a practical treatise on the analysis of tea, coffee, cocoa, chocolate, maté etc.

ISBN/EAN: 9783337423438

Printed in Europe, USA, Canada, Australia, Japan

Cover: Foto ©Andreas Hilbeck / pixelio.de

More available books at **www.hansebooks.com**

TEA, COFFEE, AND COCOA.

TEA, COFFEE, AND COCOA:

A PRACTICAL TREATISE

ON THE

ANALYSIS OF TEA, COFFEE, COCOA, CHOCOLATE, MATÉ (PARAGUAY TEA), ETC.

BY

ALFRED WANKLYN, M.R.C.S.

CORRESPONDING MEMBER OF THE ROYAL BAVARIAN ACADEMY OF SCIENCES,
PUBLIC ANALYST FOR BUCKINGHAMSHIRE, BUCKINGHAM,
AND HIGH WYCOMBE.

LONDON:

TRÜBNER & CO., 57 & 59 LUDGATE HILL.

1874.

PREFACE.

THIS book is intended to form one of a series of Manuals for the use of Public Analysts under the Adulteration Act, and in writing it I have put forward the results of my own experience and observation. For much of the material, I am, however, indebted to the labours of others. To Péligot, whose work on Tea is more than thirty years old, I am largely indebted, as will be apparent to my readers. Zöller's paper in Liebig's "Annalen" in the year 1871, I have likewise quoted. To Mr Allen of Sheffield, as will likewise be observed, I am indebted for the titration of tannin described in its proper place. The ash of coffee has likewise been investigated by Mr Allen.

The part of the book relating to Tea has been in type since the beginning of May. To this circumstance the absence of all allusion to some very recent papers by Mr Allen and Mr Wigner is to be ascribed. In a general way I regard the most recent investigations as being favourable to my views as expressed in this book.

In the part devoted to Coffee, I have largely availed myself of the report by Graham, Stenhouse, and Campbell, published by the Chemical Society in the year 1857.

In preparing the section on Cocoa and Chocolate, I have

b

received great assistance from Mr John Holm, to whose excellent lecture on Cocoa and its Manufacture, given before the Society of Arts early this year, and published in a separate form, I beg to refer my readers.

To Mr William Bettel, who has worked my new Tea-Assay in my own laboratory, and whose very careful analysis of cocoa-ash is published in Part III., I am under great obligations. The determinations of tea-extract marked W. B. were done by Mr Bettel for me.

I am the more careful to make this acknowledgment of Mr Bettel's work, since the Chemical Society has recently disgraced itself by its refusal to receive him as a Fellow; and since the Local Government Board has refused to confirm his appointment to the office of Public Analyst of Middlesborough, on the ground that his chemical ability was not sufficiently established.

It is not a novelty for either the Society or the Board to blunder; and in rejecting Mr Bettel, the Society has satirised the election of the great majority of its Fellows, and the Board the majority of its acts of confirmation.

117 CHARLOTTE STREET, FITZROY SQUARE,
LONDON, 8th July 1874.

TABLE OF CONTENTS.

———

PART II.

PART III.

PART IV.

TEA-ANALYSIS.

———◆———

CHAPTER I.

INTRODUCTION.

TEA, as it occurs in commerce, is the *prepared* leaves of the tea-plant (*Thea sinensis*); and the different varieties of tea depend chiefly on the age of the leaf at the time of gathering, and on the manner of its preparation.

The tea-plant appears to be indigenous to China, but it also flourishes in Japan and in the Himalaya. The plant is described as a shrub growing to from four to thirty feet in height, and as usually five or six feet in height.

The root of the plant is irregular and divided; the stem also divides into very numerous and irregular branches. The leaves are alternate. The flowers are white, and bear some resemblance to wild roses. They are usually about an inch in diameter. The plant is an evergreen, and the flowering is continued very far on into the winter.

The leaves present the following characters :—They bear some resemblance to the willow, being of course of various sizes. The border is serrated more regularly than the willow, but the serration just stops short of the stalk.

A

The *venation* is said to be very characteristic. The veins run out from the midrib almost parallel to one another; but before the border of the leaf is reached, they alter their course, turning so as to leave a bare space just within the border of the leaf.

In making an examination of a sample of tea, so as to ascertain whether these characters are present, it will be found convenient to pour hot water on the leaves so as to soften them, and spread them out; otherwise considerable difficulty might be experienced owing to the brittleness of the dry leaf.

The tea of commerce is not subject to much irregularity in its hygrometric condition. There is usually about 8 per cent. of moisture in it; and this may fall to 6 per cent. or rise to 10 per cent.

Tea is a complex mixture of a variety of substances. Being a leaf, it necessarily contains some woody fibre, the quantity of which, as determined by Mulder, is 17·1 per cent. in green tea, and 28·3 per cent. in black tea. According to Péligot, whose admirable investigation of tea is a chemical classic, there is also a large quantity of legumen, a nitrogenous substance which is sometimes called vegetable caseine. The percentage of this substance is given by Péligot as about 15 in tea in its usual air-dried condition. Woody fibre, legumen, together with some tannic acid, colouring matter, and a certain quantity of the ash, make up mainly the portion of the leaf which is not soluble in boiling water.

Tannic acid, probably of a peculiar kind, theine, which is the alkaloid of tea, dextrine, glucose, gum, and a portion of the ash, pass into solution when tea is infused. An essential oil, present in very small quantities, but undoubtedly very potent in its effects, passes also into the infusion.

The tea of commerce is accused of three descriptions of sophistication. It is said to be sometimes mixed with leaves which are not tea; sometimes it is sanded, and adulterated with a variety of mineral substances; and sometimes it is more or less completely spent.

Each trade has its own besetting adulteration; and, as in the milk trade the prevalent sophistications are watering and skimming, so in the tea trade the besetting malpractice is the selling of partially-exhausted tea, and the main efforts of the tea-analyst should be directed to this form of adulteration.

The mixing of foreign leaves with tea, and the mineral adulterations, are comparatively trivial; but nevertheless, the public analyst is frequently called upon to deal with them.

Foreign leaves are detected by their botanical characters, and by the absence of the special structural marks which have been already described.

Chemically, as will be explained in next chapter, an examination of the ash affords some criterea which may be utilised for the purpose of identifying the tea leaf.

Péligot has also pointed out that tea leaves differ from other leaves by their extraordinary richness in nitrogen. In different varieties of tea dried at 110° C he found—

	Percentage of Nitrogen.
Pekoe, ...	6·58
Gunpowder, ...	6·62
Souchong, ...	6·15
Assam, ...	5·10

The manufactured tea leaf is, indeed, by the process of manufacture rendered more nitrogenous than the fresh leaves of the plant. In these Péligot found 4·37 per cent. of nitrogen, the leaves having been analysed in the dry state, as dried at 100° C. During the preparation to which the leaves of the tea-plant are subjected in order to fit them for the market, a quantity of juice is expressed from them; and the rise in nitrogen in the prepared leaf is accounted for on the supposition that this juice is not so rich in nitrogen as the remainder of the leaf which is left behind.

If the tea leaf be unique in containing an exceedingly high percentage of nitrogen, it is obvious that a determination of nitrogen in tea might be useful as a method of identification, and accordingly I shall devote a portion of a chapter to a description of the determination of nitrogen in tea, and organic substances in general.

A shorter and easier operation is the determination of albuminoid ammonia in tea-extract; and moreover, the data so obtained appear to be characteristic of tea. I shall accordingly devote some space to this subject.

CHAPTER II

THE ASH.

In the common kinds of wood, such as oak, deal, &c., the proportion of ash is a few tenths per cent. Thus, taking wood in its ordinary air-dried condition, when it contains some 20 or 30 per cent. of moisture, Sprengel found 0·36 per cent. of ash in beech wood, and 0·20 per cent. of ash in the wood of the oak, and I have found 0·37 per cent. of ash in common deal.

Leaves, on the other hand, contain ten, twenty, or even thirty times as much mineral matter; and doubtless there is a connection between this abundance of mineral matter and the active chemical changes which take place in the leaves during the growth of the plant.

The following determinations of the ash in leaves dried completely at 100° C were made in my laboratory last year. The leaves were gathered towards the end of August:—

	Percentage of ash in dried leaves.
Beech, ...	4·52
Bramble, ...	4·53
Elder, ...	10·67
Gooseberry, . . .	13·50
Hawthorn, ...	8·05
Plum, ...	9·90
Willow, ...	9·34

To these may be appended determinations of the ash of Paraguay tea and of common tea, viz.—

Paraguay tea, ...	6·28
Common tea, ...	5·92

In tea, therefore, as in leaves in general, the ash amounts to a considerable percentage, and a chemical examination of the ash forms an important part of the analysis of tea.

The proportion of ash in tea is tolerably constant.

In Péligot's paper, published more than thirty years ago, the ash was given as follows :—

	Ash per cent.
Black tea (Souchong), . . .	5·5
Green tea (Gunpowder), . . .	5·5
Another kind of tea, ...	6·0
Pekoe (black), ...	5·3

A more recent investigation by Zöller (Liebig's "Annalen," May 1871) gives the ash in air-dried tea, received direct from the plantations in the Himalaya, as being 5·63 per cent. ; and my own analyses, made during the last and the present year, have furnished the following results :—

	Percentage of ash in air-dried tea.
Common tea, ...	5·63
Civil Service tea, ...	5·56
Horniman's tea, ...	5·99
Mandarin's tea (at eight shillings per lb.), ...	5·3
Orange Pekoe (at five shillings per lb.),	5·84
,, ,, ...	6·06
Green tea (four shillings and sixpence per lb.), ...	5·86
Very fine Himalayan tea ("Queen Elizabeth"), ...	5·00
Himalayan tea (Pekoe), . . .	6·06
Himalayan tea (Pekoe Souchong), .	5·37

From all which it appears that the range of variation of the ash of tea is from five to six, and that genuine tea rarely yields so little as five per cent. of ash, and rarely so much as six per cent. of ash.

The method by which the ash is determined is by incineration. A weighed quantity of the tea (from one to two grammes), in its ordinary commercial state, is burnt in a platinum crucible, and the resulting ash weighed. By observing a few simple precautions very constant and accurate results are attainable. The crucible should be clean and bright (it may be polished with charcoal-powder); the lid should fit accurately; and an iron triangle, covered with tobacco-pipe in a well-known manner, may be employed to support the crucible during the ignition. The operation is commenced by igniting the empty crucible, which is then allowed to cool, being placed for that purpose either on a clean piece of porcelain, or else on a clean piece of iron. Immediately on the crucible becoming cold, it is weighed. The one or two grammes of tea is then put into the crucible, and the crucible with its contents is then weighed. It is then ignited over either a spirit-lamp, or else a good Bunsen burner, or else in a muffle, the contents being stirred up with a platinum wire. When the ignition is complete, the crucible is covered with its lid, let cool, and then immediately weighed. If there be any doubt as to the completeness of the ignition, the crucible is again ignited; and if there be no difference in weight, the ignition is thereby proved to be complete. As will be obvious, in order to have accurate results it is an indispensable condition that the crucible should be in the same condition when it is weighed empty and when weighed charged with the ash, and this is insured by the preliminary ignition and rapid weighing as above described.

As has been mentioned, genuine tea, as brought by hand direct from China, or from the Himalaya, or such as is a fair commercial article, does not yield less than 5 per cent. of ash, or sensibly more than 6 per cent. The analyst will, however, meet with tea in commerce which contains 13 per cent. of ash, and even more than that. Such tea is sophisticated, and usually will be found to be sanded. Indeed, it is probable that the true ash of the absolutely clean tea leaf, in the ordinary air-dried condition, is about 5 per cent.; whilst the 6 per cent., or approximations to 6 per cent. of ash, which are sometimes met with, are probably due to a slight but unavoidable sanding of the leaves, which it would be exceedingly unfair to regard as an adulteration.

When the ash much exceeds 6 per cent., the first question to be answered is whether that is accidental, or whether the high yield of ash would be maintained if a large quantity of the sample were incinerated. The burning up of a large quantity of tea is inconvenient, and the following operation may be conveniently substituted for it.

50 or 100 grammes of tea is weighed out (it is quite accurate enough if the weighing be within half a gramme) and boiled with about ten times its weight of water in a porcelain dish or a wide beaker. This boiling will wash the sand off the leaves, and the sand will sink to the bottom, whilst the leaves float in the liquid. When the liquid has been allowed to cool sufficiently, the leaves may be removed with the hand, and the liquid, together with the sand, may then be poured on a filter. The sand is then to be washed, dried, ignited in a platinum dish, and weighed. In this manner the sand yielded by 50 or 100 grammes may be actually weighed.

By way of example, I will cite an analysis of a sample of Caper tea which I was called upon to examine. The percentage of ash determined upon 3 grammes of the tea was 15·49. In a second experiment 50 grammes was boiled with water, and the sand got out of the leaves washed, dried, ignited, and weighed. The sand weighed 4·181 grammes, equal to 8.362 per cent. of sand, which agrees sufficiently well with the determination of sand by the ignition-process.

The composition of the ash of genuine tea has been carefully studied. In Zöller's paper, which I have already quoted, will be found a very elaborate analysis of the ash yielded by Himalayan tea. Zöller's numbers are the following :—

Potash,	39.22
Soda,	0·65
Magnesia,	6·47
Lime,	4·24
Oxide of iron,	4·38
Protoxide of manganese,	1·03
Phosphoric acid,	14·55
Sulphuric acid,	*trace*
Chlorine,	0·81
Silica,	4·35
Carbonic acid,	24·30
	100·00

This analysis is especially important, inasmuch as the tea which furnished the ash was of guaranteed purity : and no question of the possibility of sophistication could arise.

On inspecting the analysis, it will be observed that tea-ash contains a quantity of iron, and likewise some manganese. The presence of manganese is indeed so marked in tea-ash, that on subsequent treatment of the ash with water, I have myself obtained a deep-green solution of the manganate. Owing to the manganese in it, tea-ash also always evolves chlorine very perceptibly when it is treated with hydrochloric acid.

Tea-ash is completely (or very nearly completely) soluble in hydrochloric acid. Most samples of commercial tea will, however, leave a slight insoluble residue of sand when the ash from them is subjected to the action of an acid. If necessary, this residue may be dried, ignited, and weighed. It should, of course, be trifling in amount : and here again, I cannot forbear repeating the caution not to mistake an accidental fragment of quartz in the gramme that is being incinerated for a serious adulteration of the sample.

If a sample of tea should yield *only* the normal percentage of ash, and at the same time contain a considerable quantity of silica, such a combination of characters would afford the strongest evidence of sophistication.

This will be evident, since the tea-ash is an essential part of the tea ; and if a part of the tea-ash be absent, the sample must have been deprived of at least the corresponding quantity of tea.

Spent tea leaves contain less ash than genuine tea : according to Zöller they contain 3·06 parts of ash in 100 parts of the completely dried spent leaves.

When the tea-ash is deficient, the explanation may therefore be that genuine tea has been more or less replaced by spent tea leaves.

If the analysis of tea-ash be referred to, it will be seen that a considerable proportion of the ash must be soluble in water. More than one-half of the ash should be soluble in water.

For practical purposes, I should not recommend a complete analysis of tea-ash, but I should very strongly recommend determination of the ratio of soluble to insoluble portions of the ash.

Such a determination is made by boiling the ash several

times with a little water, filtering, washing the precipitate on the filter, drying the precipitate, igniting it, and weighing it.

The weight of the insoluble part of the ash may then be subtracted from the weight of the entire ash, and in that manner both insoluble ash and soluble ash will be arrived at.

The following determinations of the quantities of "soluble ash" and "insoluble ash," in 100 parts of various kinds of completely dried leaves, will be of interest here :—

Name of leaf.	Soluble ash.	Insoluble ash.
Beech,	2·00	2·52
Bramble,	1·84	2·69
Elder,	3·19	7·48
Gooseberry,	7·83	5·67
Hawthorn,	3·78	4·27
Plum,	5·66	4·24
Willow,	4·16	5·18
Paraguay tea,	4·22	2·06
Common tea,	3·55	2·37

In spent tea leaves the ratio of soluble to insoluble ash must be very different from what it is in genuine tea. Zöller's analysis of the spent leaves shows this very strikingly. Zöller's figures are—

Potash,	7·34
Soda,	0·69
Magnesia,	11·45
Lime,	10·76
Oxide of iron,	9·53
Protoxide of manganese,	1·97
Chlorine,	trace
Phosphoric acid,	25·41
Sulphuric acid,	trace
Silica,	7·57
Carbonic acid,	25·28
	100·00

It is easy to see that an ash of this composition cannot be very soluble in water.

In conclusion, I will mention the results of an experiment of my own, made with the object of determining whether the short stalks which are met with in every sample of genuine tea differ, as to their yield of ash, from the rest of the leaf. I carefully picked out a quantity of stalk, and determined the ash in it, and found no difference between the percentage of ash in the stalks and that in the entire sample of tea.

CHAPTER III.

THE EXTRACT: AND THE TEA-ASSAY.

THE part of the tea which we really use being that which passes into the infusion—viz., the extract of tea—it is natural to look to the extract itself as affording the directest evidence of the quality and the genuineness of a sample of tea. We may regard the extract both quantitatively and qualitatively, and from the former point of view are led to the tea-assay, or determination of the weight of tea-extract which a given weight of tea is capable of yielding.

In Péligot's admirable paper on tea, we find determinations of tea-extract, the author being quite alive to the practical importance of such a test. I quote Péligot's results from his paper :—

BLACK TEA.

	Parts soluble in Boiling Water, the Tea being taken	
	Dry.	In its ordinary condition.
"Souchong fin,"	45·7	40·3
„ „	46·0	40·7
Souchong ordinaire, . . .	41·8	37·3
„ „	40·3	36·0
Pekoe, ...	34·6	31·3
„	38·1	34·5
Pekoe orange, ...	48·7	44·5
„ „	46·8	42·8

	Parts soluble in Boiling Water, the Tea being taken	
	Dry.	In its ordinary condition.
Souchong, ...	42·8	39·0
Congo, ...	40·9	36·8
Congo bon, ...	45·8	41·5
„ „	45·0	40·7
Bohea, ...	44·4	39·8
Caper, ...	39·3	35·8
Assam, ...	45·4	41·7
The Java, ...	35·2	32·7
Pekoe ordinaire, ...	41·5	38·0

GREEN TEA.

Poudre à Canon, ...	51·9	48·5
„ „	50·2	46·9
Imperial, ...	43·1	39·6
„	47·9	44·0
Hyson, ...	47·7	43·8
Hyson fin, ...	46·9	43·1
Schoulang, ...	45·9	42·3
Hyson Skin, ...	43·5	39·8
Toukay, ...	42·2	38·4

These results were arrived at by the employment of a valid, but rather inconvenient method. Péligot weighed out ten grammes of tea, boiled it with water so long as anything dissolved out, and afterwards dried up the exhausted tea leaves, drying at first at low temperatures, and then at higher temperatures, and finally weighed the exhausted leaves. The loss in weight is the weight of the tea-extract: care being taken to weigh the original tea and the exhausted tea leaves in the same state of dryness. The results, as will be observed, are stated both on the perfectly dry tea, and on the tea in its ordinary air-dried or commercial condition.

Instead of weighing tea-leaves before and after extraction, and taking the difference in weight as the weight of the extract, there is another obvious process, viz., evaporating down the extract to dryness, and weighing it. Péligot tested his method by comparing, in one or more instances, its results with results got by the other process, and found them to be concordant. I have likewise made experiments, and determined the tea-extract by both processes, and got the same result. There is, therefore, no question of the validity of the method ; but, as chemists will readily understand, it is very tedious and troublesome. The drying up of the exhausted leaves, and the getting of them into the same hygroscopic condition as the original tea, presents considerable practical difficulties.

The evaporation of the infusion to dryness, and the weighing of the dry extract, is likewise a tedious process in its unmodified state. I have accordingly set to work to effect such modifications as will render it at once easy, accurate, and rapid.

With this object in view, I have made experiments which establish the following conclusions :—

(1.) If a given quantity of tea be boiled with successive portions of water, no more tea-extract is got than if the same tea be boiled once with a large quantity of water.

(2.) I have boiled tea with 25 times its weight of water, with 50 times, with 100 times, and with 200 times its weight of water, and got as much extract with the first as with the others.

(3.) Whether the infusion is kept for a length of time just at the boiling-point, or whether the infusion be made to boil vigorously, makes some difference in the result. (Brisk boiling extracts about one-tenth more than slow boiling.)

(4.) If the boiling be **very** vigorous, half an hour's boiling is as effective as an hour's boiling.

(5.) 0·3 or 0·4 gramme of tea-extract, spread over the surface of a platinum dish capable of holding 100 c. c., dries very readily in the water-bath, and is very constant.

Founded on these observations, I now work a tea-assay as follows :—10 grammes of tea is weighed out, and introduced into a flask capable of holding about 700 c. c. Into the flask 500 c. c. of distilled water is accurately measured. A cork and bent tube is then adapted to the mouth of the flask (which should have a stout lip), and a connection is established with a small Liebig's condenser. The contents of the flask are next heated and made to boil strongly, and 50 c. c. is distilled over and collected. That having been done, the boiling is stopped, the flask and Liebig's condenser disconnected, and the 50 c. c. of distillate poured back into the flask. The decoction of tea is then to be observed carefully. If quite clear, 50 grammes (or more accurately 50·3 grammes) are weighed out and evaporated to dryness in the water-bath, and weighed till constant.

If the decoction be not quite clear (which most frequently happens), then it is to be filtered hot. The first small portion of filtrate is best thrown away; and then 50·3 grammes of filtrate is collected, weighed, and dried up in the water-bath until the residual tea-extract becomes constant.

The weighing out of the 50·3 grammes of decoction whilst still hot presents no real difficulties, inasmuch as the weighing error through heating does not amount to more than one or two centigrammes in such a case. For this purpose a rough balance (whose performance, however, has been tested) will answer very well.

As will also be obvious, there would be no great difficulty in contriving a measure to hold a little more than 50 c. c., and which would contain approximately 50·3 grammes of the hot decoction.

Having done the operation in the manner directed, the weight of the tea-extract actually weighed will be the weight of the tea-extract yielded by one gramme of the sample to be assayed.

The entire operation may be performed under two hours.

The following determinations have been made in my laboratory :—

		Percentage of tea-extract in air-dried sample.
Specimen of tea direct from China,	(1.)	41·7
	(2.)	40·2
	(3.)	41·2
Himalayan tea ("Queen Elizabeth")		38·6
Himalayan tea (Pekoe Souchong)		35·4
„ „ another sample	W.B.	39·9
Java tea (5s. 6d. per lb.)	W.B.	40·8
Caper tea (4s. per lb.)	W.B.	37·6
Young Hyson (4s. per lb.)	W.B.	42·0
Choice Gunpowder (4s. per lb.)	W.B.	46·3

The above are either high-priced or else extraordinary teas.

B

CHAPTER IV.

"FREE AND ALBUMINOID" AMMONIA IN TEA-EXTRACT. ESTIMATION OF NITROGEN IN TEA.

TEA-EXTRACT yields a comparatively large quantity of ammonia when it is boiled with potash and permanganate of potash, and it is probable that this character may prove very valuable in the testing of tea.

In order to make these determinations, I operate as follows:—First, a suitable infusion is prepared by boiling 5 grammes of the sample of tea with 500 c. c. of water (*vide* chapter iii.), and filling up to the 500 c. c.

Of this infusion 5 or 10 c. c. (equal to the extract from 50 or 100 milligrammes of tea) is a convenient quantity to take.

A solution of potash, containing about 10 per cent. of solid potash, and free from ammonia and nitrogenous matter, is required, and may be easily obtained.

10 c. c. of this solution of potash having been put into a small flask-retort working in an oil-bath, and connected with a small Liebig's condenser, the whole apparatus is to be carefully freed from the last traces of ammonia, which is accomplished by simply distilling a little water through it. That having been done, 5 or 10 c. c. of the tea-infusion are poured into the retort, which is corked up and heated in the oil-bath to 150° C.

Having been maintained for a short time at that temperature, it is lifted out of the bath; some 50 c. c. of pure water are poured into the retort, which is again heated in the oil-bath. More than half of the water is then distilled over, and in this manner the "free ammonia" is obtained in the distillate.

When this has been done, 50 c. c. of potash and permanganate solution (strength 200 grm. of KHO, and 8 grm. $KMnO_4$ in the litre) is added to the contents of the retort, and distilled so as to yield a distillate containing the "albuminoid ammonia."

On making experiments with infusion of tea, it appeared that the sum of "free" and "albuminoid" ammonia, obtained as described, did not differ materially from the albuminoid ammonia obtained *at once* by boiling the infusion with potash and permanganate.

My results are as follows. The extract from 100 milligrammes of tea gave—

Free ammonia, .	0·28	milligrammes.
Albuminoid ammonia, .	0·43	,,
Total,	0·71	,,

And in another experiment, in which I omitted to take free and albuminoid ammonia in separate operations, but proceeded at once to get albuminoid ammonia, from 100 milligrammes of tea the extract yielded—(Total) Albuminoid ammonia, 0·70 milligrammes.

These experiments are made with very great ease, and I confidently recommend this method of investigating the strength of tea-infusion. (For the details of the method of measuring ammonia, *vide* "Water-Analysis.")

For comparison with tea-infusion, I am at present able to cite only two examples—viz., infusion of gooseberry leaves and infusion of Paraguay tea.

The extract from 100 milligrammes of gooseberry leaves gave—

Free ammonia, . .	0·20	milligrammes
Albuminoid ammonia .	0·295	,,
Total,	0·495	,,

The extract from 100 milligrammes of gooseberry leaves gave also, total ammonia, not distinguished into free and albuminoid—(Total) Albuminoid ammonia, 0·45 milligrammes. Paraguay tea gave, from 100 milligrammes—(Total) Albuminoid ammonia, 0·50 milligrammes. From which it appears that tea leaves yield an extraordinary amount of ammonia when the extract is submitted to the "ammonia-process." As has already been remarked in the introductory chapter, tea is remarkably rich in nitrogen, so much so, that a determination of nitrogen may be resorted to as a means of identification.

Such a determination may be made by the well-known Gay Lussac method, which I will now describe.

The sample of tea must first of all be well mixed up. With this object it is well to take several grammes and powder them in a mortar, and of this tea-powder some 0·3 grammes should be accurately weighed out. This is to be mixed with some 50 grammes of oxide of copper, which has been oxidised *without* the employment of nitric acid, and which shortly before use had been ignited and allowed to cool.

A combustion-tube of hard German glass, which is closed at one end and perfectly clean, is then charged as follows :—

At the closed end a layer, some three or four inches in length, of a mixture of dry bicarbonate of soda and fused bichromate of potash. This mixture is intended to give out carbonic acid. Next to this mixture come some two inches of oxide of copper, then the mixture of tea and oxide of copper, then more oxide of copper, then clean metallic copper, then a perforated cork and exit tube which dips under mercury. The combustion-tube is placed in an appropriate furnace. By heating the layer of carbonate of soda and bichromate of potash, carbonic acid is caused to traverse the tube and to expel the air from it. This having been done, the tube is heated gradually from before backwards, so as to burn up the tea. The gases are collected over mercury. At the end of the operation carbonic acid is once more made to traverse the tube by again heating the mixture at the back, and all the nitrogen is driven from the tube and collected. Finally the carbonic acid is absorbed by means of potash, and the residual nitrogen gas is measured with well-known precautions. The gas should also be tested for binoxide of nitrogen by means of oxygen and pyrogallate of potash. Any binoxide of nitrogen gas must be measured and allowed for.

CHAPTER V

THEINE.

TEA and coffee contain one and the same alkaloid, to which the names caffeine and theine have been given. The formula of this alkaloid is

$$C_8H_{10}N_4O_2.$$

It was first discovered under the name of caffeine in 1820 by Runge, who got it from coffee. Seven years later Oudry discovered a crystalline substance—which he extracted from tea, and to which he gave the name theine. Jobst and Mulder afterwards showed that the active principle extracted from tea was identical with caffeine. By Pfaff and Liebig the formula of the alkaloid was settled.

Theine is a substance which crystallises very beautifully, forming white silk-like crystals, containing an atom of water of crystallisation. The specific gravity of the crystals is 1·23 at 19° C. The water of crystallisation is not altogether driven off by a temperature of 150° C. At 178° C. theine melts, and at 185° C. it sublimes.

As deposited from aqueous solutions, theine contains an atom of water of crystallisation (formula $C_8H_{10}N_4O_2 + H_2O$); but as deposited from solution in alcohol or in ether, or when sublimed, it is anhydrous. It is much more soluble in hot water than in cold water, or in alcohol or ether. According to Péligot, one part of theine dissolves in 300 parts of ether, and one part of **theine dissolves in 93 parts of** water at ordinary temperatures. It is a base of the same class as aniline and urea; that is to say, it combines with acids yielding crystalline compounds, **but it never neutralises an acid.** When aqueous solutions of its salts are boiled, they suffer spontaneous decomposition, as a rule, and deposit theine. With chloride of platinum, chloride of gold, corrosive sublimate, the hydrochlorate of theine enters **into** combination, forming a double salt **with each.**

Solutions of theine are precipitated by tannin, yielding a white tannate of theine which contains 41·9 parts of theine, and 58·1 parts of tannin. In tea the theine exists in combination with tannin.

As will be manifest from its formula, theine is one **of the** most highly nitrogenous substances known to **chemists, its** percentage composition **being—**

C_8	96	49·48
H_{10}	10	5·16
N_4	56	28·87
O_2	32	16·49
	194	100·00

Connected **with its high percentage** of nitrogen **(almost** double of **that found in the albuminous** substances) is its property of yielding **abundance of** cyanides when fused with soda-lime.

According to Rochleder, this property of yielding a cyanide distinguishes theine from a number of organic bases—viz., piperine, morphine, quinine, and cinchonine.

A cyanogen compound, chloride of cyanogen, is likewise produced by the action of chlorine upon theine.

With the **base of cocoa, which has received the name**

theobromine, theine is closely related, being methylated theobromine. Strecker has, in point of fact, produced theine from theobromine. This he accomplished by acting upon a silver-derivative of theobromine with iodide of methyl in a sealed tube heated to 100° C. : the reaction being as follows :—

Silver Theobromine.

$$\overbrace{C_7H_7N_4O_2Ag} \qquad +CH_3I = Ag\,I$$

Theine.

$$+ \quad \overbrace{C_8H_{10}N_4O_2}$$

Little more is, however, known of the structure of theine and theobromine. These bodies are apparently related to uric acid, inasmuch as, like it, when exposed to the successive action of nitric acid and ammonia, they yield a purple colouring-matter (Murexide).

As has been said, theine exists in tea, not in the free state, but in the form of tannate of theine, which appears to be dissolved by the excess of tannic acid contained by the tea leaf, and so it comes to pass that the theine makes its appearance in the infusion, instead of remaining behind in the exhausted leaves.

The proportion of theine in tea has been variously given by different chemists. Mulder found 0·43 per cent. in green tea, and 0·46 per cent. in black tea. Stenhouse found 1·05 and 0·98 in green tea, and 1·02 and 1·27 in black tea. Péligot found 2·34 and 3·0 per cent. of theine in tea; and Zöller, whose research is comparatively recent (*vide* Liebig's "Annalen" for 1871) found 4·94 per cent. of theine in Himalayan tea.

It would be a mistake to regard these varying results as showing that the quantity of theine in tea is very variable.

They only illustrate the difficulties which stand in the way of a quantitative extraction of the theine, and the imperfection of the earlier methods. In Péligot's paper these difficulties are referred to, and by making an attempt to extract the theine from a sample of tea the chemist will easily acquire a sense of the reality of them.

The following is a description of the method for the extraction of the theine :—

A quantity of tea is boiled with a considerable quantity of water—viz., 200 grammes of tea with 3 litres of water. The infusion is then to be squeezed out of the leaves, which are to be boiled with a fresh quantity of water, and again subjected to pressure. This is to be repeated a third time. The several portions of infusion squeezed out of the leaves are mixed together, and treated with excess of acetate of lead and ammonia, which precipitates the tannin and the colouring-matter. The liquid is next to be filtered. The filtrate is then evaporated down to a small bulk, first over the naked flame, and afterwards in the water-bath. On being allowed to cool, the solution will deposit crude theine, which is removed by filtration. The filtrate is afterwards nearly dried up in the water-bath, and the residue boiled with alcohol, which dissolves the theine out of it. From its hot alcoholic solution theine crystallises on cooling.

A final purification may be effected by crystallisation from ether, and decolourizing with animal charcoal.

As will have been perceived, the extraction of theine will need improvement and simplification before it can be of much value to the food-analyst in his investigation of samples of tea.

CHAPTER VI.

A LARGE proportion of tea-extract consists of tannin, and in green tea there is much more tannin than in black tea. This difference depends upon the circumstance that part of the tannin originally existing in the leaf is destroyed during the process of fermentation which takes place in the preparation to which black tea is subjected in the process of manufacture.

In green tea there is, according to Allen (*vide Chemical News*, vol. 29, p. 189), about 20 per cent. of tannin ; but the quantity is subject to great variation. In black tea, according to the same authority, the tannin amounts to 10 per cent. on the average, the extremes being 12·00 and 9·50 per cent.

For the estimation of the tannin various processes are in use. There is a titration by means of a standard solution of gelatine, which depends upon the well-known property possessed by gelatine of forming insoluble compounds with tannin. This titration is not easy, and is admitted to be very tedious by those who have employed it. A much more promising method, recently described by Mr Allen (*vide Chemical News*, vol. 29, pp. 169 and 189), consists in titrating by means of standard solution of lead, the point of saturation being indicated by the red colour struck by an ammoniacal solution of ferricyanide of potassium. The standard solution of lead is made by dissolving 5 grammes of acetate of lead in water, which is diluted so as to measure a litre. This solution is filtered if necessary.

The indicator is made by dissolving 5 milligrammes of crystals of ferricyanide of potassium in 5 c. c. of water, and mixing that with 5 c. c. of strong ammonia. One drop of this solution is capable of colouring one milligramme of tannin dissolved in 100 c. c. of water.

The exact strength of the solution of lead is ascertained by trial with a standard solution of tannin.

In using the solution of lead, 10 c. c. of it are first diluted with nine times their volume of water. The tea-infusion is then dropped into it from a graduated burette, until the liquid strikes a red with a drop of the indicator. Before using the indicator a little of the solution is filtered, and the filtrate allowed to drop on filter-paper, moistened with a drop of the indicator.

The infusion of tea is made by boiling 2 grammes of tea with water, and afterwards diluting to 250 c. c. ; and it will of course be understood that the smaller the quantity of this infusion required to saturate the 10 c. c. of lead solution, the higher the percentage of tannin in the sample of tea. Mr Allen considers that this test is specially applicable for ascertaining whether black tea has been mixed with spent tea. Taking the normal percentage of tannin in genuine black tea as 10, and the percentage of tannin in spent tea as 2, he proposes the following formula for the calculation of the percentage of spent tea in the sample :—

$$E = \frac{(10-T)\ 100}{8}$$

where E = percentage of spent tea and T = percentage of tannin found in the sample.

CHAPTER VII.

CALCULATION OF RESULTS.

In coming to a judgment as to the genuineness of a sample of tea of which an analysis has been made, it is of importance to bear in mind that genuine tea is subject to considerable variation in composition. The condition of the leaf at the time of gathering, and the different treatments to which it is subjected in the process of manufacture—differences which determine whether the tea shall be black tea or green tea—cause the composition of tea to exhibit a wide range of variation.

Taking the percentage of tea-extract as the basis from which to start, we observe that in genuine tea this may range from 32 up to about 50 per cent. ; that is to say, unsophisticated tea, in its ordinary air-dried condition, may yield up to the action of boiling water from 32 to 50 per cent. of its weight.

Such being the case, it is obvious that a determination of the percentage of extract will not enable the analyst to say whether the sample of tea consists of the lower variety of genuine tea, or whether it consists partly of the higher variety of genuine tea and partly of spent tea. In a general way, however, this is a question the solution of which is not of much importance to the public analyst.

A little assistance, in such a case, may be derived from a

determination of the soluble ash, which would probably be found to be rather deficient. Although tea may be exceptionally rich in extract, and although there are difficulties in the way of deciding whether a given specimen of tea consists of average tea or of rich tea mixed with spent tea, there are no such difficulties in recognising the case of average tea mixed with considerable quantities of spent tea. For this purpose it will be convenient to employ the formula :—

$$E = \frac{(32-R)\ 100}{30}$$

where E is the percentage of spent tea in the sample, and R the percentage of tea-extract found by the tea-assay.

From an examination of the ash, data are obtained which may be utilised in the following formula :—

$$E = (6-2S)\ 20$$

E being the percentage of spent tea, and S the percentage of soluble ash in the tea. This formula was proposed by Mr Allen, and is based upon the determinations of soluble ash brought out by me, and supplemented by Mr Allen's determination that the soluble ash in spent tea is 0·5 per cent.

It is assumed in this formula that the soluble ash in genuine tea is 3·0 per cent., and in spent tea 0·5 per cent.

From the determination of tannin, as given in last chapter, the following formula has been proposed by Mr Allen :—

$$E = \frac{(10-T)\ 100}{8}$$

In using these formulæ, it will of course be understood that the results are only rough approximations to the truth, and great judgment and discrimination is required.

Of the other forms of sophistication, mineral adulteration will be dealt with through the ash, and adulteration with foreign leaves will show itself when the tea is examined botanically. Deficient nitrogen, deficient ammonia, and deficient theine, are all indicative of foreign leaves.

PART II.

COFFEE.

COFFEE is a seed which grows in a pod, like the pea or the bean. The plant which produces coffee is a tree, *Caffea arabica*. It grows in Arabia, Ceylon, the West Indies, Brazil, and other hot countries. Before it is imported to Europe the coffee is deprived of the pod, and also of another covering.

In commerce coffee is met with in three conditions—viz., raw or unroasted, roasted, and ground. As might be imagined, it is in this last condition that it is liable to the chief sophistications.

According to Payen, 100 parts of raw coffee contain 34 parts of cellulose, 12 of water, from 10 to 13 of fat, 15·5 of dextrine, glucose, and an organic acid, 10 of legumen, 3 of indefinite organic nitrogenous substances, and 3·5 to 5 of double caffetannate of caffeine and potash.

In addition to the foregoing, Payen describes some 0·8 per cent. of free caffeine, and very small quantities of essential and aromatic oils, amounting to only 0·003 per cent. of the coffee.

Payen's determination of the ash of coffee was too high, and need not be quoted.

Within the last few months Mr Allen has published some determinations of the ash of coffee (*vide Chemical News,* vol. 25, p. 140). He finds—

		Percentage of ash.
Specimen 1,	. . . . . .	3·86
„ 2,	. . . . . .	3·95
„ 3,	. . . . . .	4·20
	Mean	4·00

and adopting my plan of investigation, he has also determined the ratio of soluble to insoluble ash, and finds that the 4 parts of ash consist of—

Soluble in water,	. . . . .	3·24
Insoluble, .	. . . . . .	0·76
		4·00

This agrees very well with the analyses of coffee-ash which have been published, and according to which rather more than half of the entire ash consists of potash in combination with carbonic and phosphoric acids; whilst the magnesia amounts to about 8 per cent., and the lime to about 4 per cent. of the entire ash. It is said that soda and silica are absent from coffee-ash, and great stress has been laid on this circumstance.

The ash of chicory (which is the main adulterant of coffee), has likewise received attention from Mr Allen. It amounts to 5·06 per cent. of the chicory, and consists of—

Soluble in water,	. . . . .	1·74
Insoluble, .	. . . . . .	3·32
		5·06

from which it may be easily understood that an examination of the ash would suffice to distinguish between coffee and chicory.

As has been said, coffee is met with raw, roasted and ground. With the raw coffee and with the simply roasted coffee, the public analyst will have very little to do, and his services will be chiefly required in dealing with ground coffee.

In the process of roasting, coffee undergoes certain changes. Before being roasted it contains from 5·7 to 7·8 per cent. of sugar, but after roasting, the percentage of sugar is not higher than 1·1, and sometimes it is even zero. (*Vide* Graham, Stenhouse, and Campbell on Coffee in the *Quarterly Journal of the Chemical Society*, vol. ix., p. 33.)

It appears, therefore, that the description of sugar which is present in raw coffee suffers destruction during roasting.

A change in the condition of the fat of coffee is also brought about by the roasting; for, whereas ether extracts with readiness only some 4 or 5 per cent. of fat from raw coffee-beans, it extracts easily double that quantity from roasted coffee. So striking is this that Von Bibra has even credited the roasting with the production of the fat, but most probably the action is only mechanical in bursting the fat-cells, and thereby rendering the fat accessible to the solvent action of the ether.

Roasted coffee is tolerably rich in nitrogen. It contains from 2·5 to 3·0 per cent. of nitrogen. This, as will be observed, is only about half as much as exists in tea (*Vide* Part I., chapter I.)

The operation of roasting tends to make coffee soluble in boiling water. Thus when raw coffee is perfectly exhausted by means of boiling water, it yields up 25 per cent., which pass into solution. Roasted coffee, on the other hand, when completely exhausted by means of boiling water, yields up 39 per cent. (Vogel). These numbers appear to be rather high.

In actually using coffee as a beverage, we are not in the habit of making anything like a complete extraction, and only some 10 or 12 per cent. of the coffee passes into the liquid.

Coffee is quite devoid of starch.

From the foregoing it will be perceived that the chemical characters of coffee provide tolerably satisfactory criteria for the recognition of many species of adulteration.

The absence of starch in genuine coffee offers in itself a character which enables us at once to deal with a whole class of possible adulterants, including every species of grain.

The absence of more than traces of sugar in roasted coffee can likewise be turned to excellent account; inasmuch as chicory, which like coffee contains no starch, is highly saccharine even after roasting.

The percentage of sugar in roasted coffee ranges from $0\cdot0$ to $1\cdot14$; in roasted chicory, on the other hand, the percentage of sugar ranges from 12 to 18.

By the aid of the copper-reduction test this character may be easily brought out.

For this purpose a standard solution of copper is required, which may be prepared by dissolving $34\cdot65$ grammes of crystallised sulphate of copper in 200 c.c. of water, and adding to it 173 grammes of double tartrate of potash and soda and 480 c.c. of solution of caustic soda (sp. gr. $1\cdot14$), the whole being subsequently diluted with water so as to occupy exactly a litre. This standard solution of copper prepared in this manner is of such a strength that 10 c.c. are reduced by $\cdot050$ gramme of grape sugar ($C_6H_{12}O_6$).

The best way of using this solution is by taking a known volume of it, say 10 c.c. accurately measured out, diluting with three or four times its volume of water, boiling and then dropping into the boiling copper-solution the sugar-solution which is to be added, until the point is just reached when the copper-solution is exhausted. As the reduction of the copper-salt, to the state of red suboxide of copper progresses, the precipitate will accumulate, and at the same time the blue colour will fade from the solution. The last delicate reading is finally effected by help of the reaction between ferrocyanide of potassium and copper-solutions; and for that purpose a little of the liquid is filtered, acidified slightly with acetic acid, and tested with a drop of solution of ferrocyanide of potassium.

In this titration, as in all like cases, the piece of advice may be given, to make a rough and rapid estimation first, and then in a second operation, when the quantity is approximately known, to make a delicate and careful reading of the exact point.

If 100 parts of coffee when infused yield sensibly more than one per cent. of sugar, then chicory may be very strongly suspected: and a rough calculation of the quantity present may be made thus :—

$$E = \frac{(S-1)\,100}{14}$$

Where in E is the percentage of chicory in the sample, and S the percentage of sugar.

The circumstance that coffee-extract is devoid, or almost devoid of sugar, whilst many other natural products yield saccharine extracts, makes itself manifest in many ways. The specific gravity of an infusion of coffee is very much lower than the specific gravity of an infusion of chicory, made from an equal weight of chicory. The following are the specific

gravities of infusion of a number of substances, as determined by Graham, Stenhouse, and Campbell in 1857.

The solutions were made by taking one part of the substance
(which had been roasted) and ten times its weight of cold
water, and then heating gradually to boiling, and filtering
through paper. The specific gravities of the solutions prepared in this manner were taken at 60° Fahr.

Spent tan,	1·0021
Lupin seed,	1·0057
Acorns,	1·0073
Peas,	1·0073
Mocha coffee,	1·0080
Beans,	1·0084
Neilgherry coffee,	1·0084
Plantation Ceylon coffee,	1·0087
Java coffee,	1·0087
Jamaica coffee,	1·0087
Costa Rica coffee,	1·0090
,, ,,	1·0090
Native Ceylon coffee,	1·0090
Brown malt,	1·0109
Parsnips,	1·0143
Carrots,	1·0171
Bouka,	1·0185
Yorkshire chicory,	1·0191
Black malt,	1·0212
Turnips,	1·0214
Rye meal,	1·0216
English chicory,	1·0217
Dandelion root,	1·0219
Red beet,	1·0221
Foreign chicory,	1·0226
Guernsey chicory,	1·0232
Mangold Wurzel,	1·0235
Maize,	1·0253
Bread raspings,	1·0263

Chicory has much greater colouring power than coffee, and

this character may be rendered available. One part of the sample is boiled with 2000 parts of water, and the solution cooled and compared with a standard colour, in a manner which will be at once intelligible to persons who are in the habit of using the Nessler-test. Graham, Stenhouse, and Campbell have also published an investigation into the colouring power of a number of substances. I cannot do better than quote the results.

Name of substance which was roasted and then treated with 2000 times its weight of boiling water.	Volume of solution required to give equal colouration.
Caramel, ...	1·00
Mangold Wurzel, ...	1·66
Bouka (coffee substitute), . . .	1·66
Black malt, ...	1·82
White turnips, ...	2·00
Carrots, ...	2·00
Chicory (dark Yorkshire), . . .	2·22
Parsnips, ...	2·50
Maize, ...	2·86
Rye, ...	2·86
Dandelion, ...	3·33
Red beet, ...	3·33
Bread raspings, ...	3·64
Acorns, ...	5·00
Over-roasted coffee, ...	5·46
High-roasted coffee, ...	5·77
Medium-roasted coffee, . . .	6·95
Coffee, ...	6·66
White Lupin seeds, ...	10·00
Peas, ...	13·33
Beans, ...	13·33
Spent Tan, ...	33·00
Brown malt, ...	40.0

In this table, the greater the volume of the solution the less the colouring power of the substance. The numbers are, therefore, inversely as the colouring powers of the different substances.

The above solutions were made by heating to 212° Fahr. : but if solutions be made at ordinary temperatures, there is a far greater difference between coffee and chicory.

Not only does chicory colour water more deeply than coffee, but it colours with far greater rapidity. No doubt the oil contained in coffee hinders the solution of the colouring matter by water, and more especially by cold water ; whereas chicory, which contains no oil, imparts its colouring matter to water with great readiness. All this tends to render the colour-test, when properly applied, especially available for the detection of chicory in coffee.

With regard to propriety of selling chicory with coffee, the remark may be made that it is certainly not right to sell a mixture of coffee with chicory under the name of pure coffee. It would, furthermore, not be unreasonable to compel the vendor to specify, approximately, the proportion of chicory contained in the mixture which is sold. This is especially desirable, inasmuch as chicory is far cheaper than coffee, and it is, therefore, necessary to protect the public against having chicory passed off for coffee.

But whilst admitting all this, I think it cannot be doubted that the mixing of chicory with coffee is really demanded by public taste, and that this admixture is made, for the most part, in order to meet the requirements of the public, and not with fraudulent intent of any kind.

The use of chicory along with coffee was originally a Dutch practice, and dates back about a century ago. For many years the nature of chicoried coffee was kept a secret by the Dutch dealers ; but in the year 1801 the secret was disclosed.

At the present time the consumption of chicory has assumed colossal proportions, and in France alone the annual consumption of chicory is 6,000,000 kilogrammes (six thousand tons approximately). In short, there is no manner of doubt that public taste demands the admixture of chicory with coffee.

Although, however, such admixtures be demanded, yet it appears to be impossible to replace coffee altogether; and elaborate attempts made by the French during the war in the early part of this century were unsuccessful in providing any substitute for coffee.

The following analyses of the ash of coffee, chicory, and of certain other seeds and roots, are quoted from the report by Graham, Stenhouse, and Campbell (*Quarterly Journal of the Chemical Society*, vol. ix., p. 46, *for the year* 1857).

ASH OF COFFEE.

	PLANTATION CEYLON.	NATIVE CEYLON.	JAVA.	COSTA RICA.	JAMAICA.	MOCHA.	NEILGHERRY.
Potash,	55·10	52·72	54·00	53·20	53·72	51·52	55·80
Soda,	...	...	...	...	...	...	...
Lime,	4·10	4·58	4·11	4·61	6·16	5·87	5·68
Magnesia,	8·42	8·46	8·20	8·66	8·37	8·87	8·49
Sesquioxide of Iron,	0·45	0·98	0·73	0·63	0·44	0·44	0·61
Sulphuric acid,	3·62	4·48	3·49	3·82	3·10	5·26	3·09
Chlorine,	1·11	0·45	0·26	1·00	0·72	0·59	0·60
Carbonic acid,	17·47	16·93	18·13	16·34	16·54	16·98	14·92
Phosphoric acid,	10·36	11·60	11·05	10·80	11·13	10·15	10·85
Silica,	...	...	...	...	...	...	...
Sand,	...	...	...	...	...	...	...
	100·63	100·20	99·97	99·06	100·18	99·68	100·04

ASH OF CHICORY.

	Darkest English (Yorkshire).	English.	Foreign.	Guernsey.
Potash,	33·48	24·88	29·56	32·07
Soda,	8·12	15·10	2·04	3·81
Lime,	9·38	9·60	5·00	5·31
Magnesia,	5·27	7·22	3·42	3·85
Sesquioxide of Iron,	3·81	3·13	5·32	3·52
Sulphuric acid,	10·29	10·53	5·38	6·01
Chlorine,	4·93	4·68	3·23	4·56
Carbonic acid,	1·78	2·88	2·80	3·19
Phosphoric acid,	10·66	11·27	7·06	6·65
Silica,	3·81	2·61	12·75	10·52
Sand,	9·32	8·08	23·10	20·19
	100·85	99·98	99·66	99·68

	LUPINS.	ACORNS.	MAIZE.	PARSNIPS.	DANDELION ROOT.
Potash,	33·54	54·93	30·74	56·54	17·95
Soda,	17·75	0·63	...	...	30·95
Lime,	7·75	6·01	3·06	6·85	11·43
Magnesia,	6·18	4·32	14·72	6·49	1·31
Sesquioxide of Iron,	...	0·54	0·84	0·53	1·27
Chlorine,	2·11	2·51	0·50	2·09	3·84
Sulphuric acid,	6·80	4·79	4·13	4·07	2·37
Carbonic acid,	0·56	13·69	...	11·44	6·21
Phosphoric acid,	25·53	11·15	44·50	13·84	11·21
Silica, &c.,	0·87	1·01	1·78	0·57	11·26
	101·09	99·58	100·27	102·42	97·80

PART III.

———◆———

COCOA AND CHOCOLATE.

Cocoa, in its various forms, and chocolate, are preparations of the seed of the cacao, or chocolate-tree, a tree which grows in hot countries.

This tree, Theobroma cacao, was cultivated in ancient Mexico; and from the ancient Mexican civilisation we derive both the use of cocoa and chocolate, and also the names by which they are called in modern times.

The tree is at present cultivated in Mexico, the West Indies, South America, and Africa. It is an evergreen, growing from fifteen to forty feet in height. The seeds are found in pods, containing twenty to forty seeds in a pod. Before leaving the country where they grow they are *cured*, as it is called. In this process a kind of fermentation is set up, which is allowed to proceed to a certain point, and then stopped.

In the year 1520 cocoa was brought to Europe by Columbus, but the earliest record of its employment in England is in the year 1659.

In modern England it is of considerable commercial importance, as the following figures testify. The quantity of raw cocoa imported into England for home consumption in

1820, was 276,321 lbs., and in 1873 it had risen to 8,311,023 lbs.

The seeds of the cacao, as they are seen in this country after importation, have the general appearance of almonds. They are brown in colour, and consist of a thin outer shell, and a more massive interior termed the *nib*. The shell is prolonged in the form of thin septa into the inner part of the seed. The relative proportions of shell and nib are approximately as 1 : 8, the nib being much the more abundant.

They vary considerably in size. Single seeds may be picked out which weigh as much as 2·7 grammes, but the average weight is much less, viz., 1·2 grammes.

Having, through the kindness of Mr Holm, obtained possession of authentic specimens of the chief varieties of cacao seeds at present in the market, I have made the following determinations of the weights of the different sorts of seeds :—

Names of Cocoa.	Weight of 100 Seeds Grammes.
Common Trinidad,	98·
Fair good Trinidad,	123·2
Very fine Trinidad,	178·7
Medium Grenada,	104·5
Fine Grenada,	131.
Caracas,	130·3
Dominican,	110·
Fine Surinam,	122.
Fine Surinam (small)	71·5
Bahia (Brazil),	118·
Mexican,	136·5
African,	128·

The following analysis of the seeds may be quoted from Mr Holm's admirable lecture delivered to the Society of Arts·

	Lampedits.	Tuchen.	Payen.	Johnson.	Playfair and Lankester.	Miller.	Boussingault.	Mitscherlich.		Myter.	Average of several other Analyses.
Fat (Cocoa Butter)	53·10	36·97	52·00	51·00	50·00	56·00	44·00	49·00	45·00	42·67	50·00
Albuminoid Substances	18·70	...	20·00	...	20·00	17·00	20·00	18·00	13·00	...	18·00
Albumin	...	...	...	...	...	...	...	...	...	...	...
Fibrin	...	30·20	...	20·00	...	...	...	...	...	12·21	...
Gluten	...	4·14	...	...	...	...	...	...	...	...	...
Extractive matter	...	...	...	...	...	...	...	18·00	0·60	...	...
Sugar	10·91	0·55	10·00	22·00	7·00	22·00*	6·00	...	14·00	19·03	10·00
Starch	7·75	0·69	...	...	6·00	...	6·00	...	...	6·40	8·00
Gum	0·90	...	...	...	...	...	13·00	...	...	...	...
Lignine	...	30·00	...	...	4·00	...	...	...	6·08	...	...
Cellulose	...	...	...	...	2·00	...	11·00	5·00	3·05	5·95	2·60
Woody Fibre	...	...	2·00	...	5·00	...	2·00	6·30	5·06	3·96	6·00
Colouring Matter	2·01	6·61	traces	...	2·00	...	4·00	1·50	1·02	5·98	1·50
Water	5·20	6·01	10·00	5·00	4·00	...	...	...	...	0·90	...
Theobromine	...	0·56	2·00	2·00	2·00	1·50	2·00	...	...	...	...
Salts	...	3·00	4·00	...	4·00	...	4·00	...	3·05	2·90	3·60
Ash	...	...	...	...	...	...	...	...	...	...	...
Humic Acid	...	7·25	...	...	...	...	...	...	...	...	...
Parts unaccounted for	1·43	1·02	...	...	...	3·50	...	...	9·14	...	0·30
Total	100·00	100·00	100·00	100 00	100·00	100·00	100·00	...	100·00	100·00	100·00

From this, it will be seen that the most abundant constituent of the seed is the fat, or cocoa butter, which constitutes about half of the entire seed. Owing, no doubt, to this circumstance, the specific gravity of the seeds is less than unity, and the seeds float on water : after being kept for some days in contact with the water, some of the fat makes its escape from the seed, which sinks down to the bottom.

I attach great importance to the determination of the ash. The following determinations of ash have been recently made in my laboratory :—

	Percentage of Ash.
Common Trinidad, ...	3·37
Very fine Trinidad, ...	3·62
Fair good fine Trinidad, ...	3·64
Fine Grenada, ...	3·12
Medium Grenada, ...	3·06
Caracas, ...	4·58
Bahia (Brazil), ...	3·31
Fine Surinam, ...	3·06
Fine Surinam (Small), ...	3·15
Mexican, ...	4·27
Dominican, ...	2·82
African, ...	2·68
The mean of the 12 being	3.39

Separate determinations of the ash of the nib and the shell have also been made.

In the nib of the Caracas, the ash amounted to 3·95 per cent., whereof 2·00 was soluble in water, and 1·95 insoluble in water.

In the nib of the Mexican seeds, the ash was found to be 2·59 per cent. : whereof 0·89 was soluble, and 1·70 insoluble in water. The shell (which, as mentioned above, forms only a very small proportion of the entire seed) is much richer in mineral matter or ash. I have found as much as 7.81 per cent. of ash in the shell. The composition of the ash of the shell is very different from that of the nib; whilst the ash of the shell is rich in carbonates, that of the nib is almost devoid of carbonates.

A very careful analysis of the ash of the entire seed has been recently made by my friend, Mr William Bettel, in my laboratory. The results are as follows :—

Composition of Ash of the entire seeds (Caracas).

Potash K_2O	29·81
Chloride of Sodium Na Cl . . .	6·10
Peroxide of Iron Fi_2O_3	1·60
Alumina, Al_2O_3	2·40
Lime, Ca O	7·72
Magnesia, Mg O	7·90
Phosphoric Acid P_2O_5	24·28
Sulphuric Acid, SO_3	1·92
Carbonic Acid, CO_2	0·98
Silica, Si O_2	5·00
Sand	12·15
	99·86

From this analysis it is apparent that the main constituent of the ash is phosphate of potash, and that there is almost total absence of carbonates. The ash of the shell being, as has been said, highly charged with carbonates, it follows that, in obtaining the ash of the entire seed, we cause the phosphates of the nib to decompose the carbonates of the shell, and so obtain an ash devoid of carbonates.

The large proportion of phosphate of potash in cocoa (certainly not far short of one per cent. in the cacao seed of good quality) is worthy the attention of the physician, and no doubt gives an especial value to a dietary consisting largely of cocoa. It will further be observed that the fine kinds of cacao seed are rich in phosphate of potash.

In making analyses of the various preparations of the cacao seed, considerable use may be made of the determination of ash, as will be explained by and by.

The Theobromine is the alkaloid of cocoa. Its formula is—

$$C_7 \ H_8 \ N_4 \ O_2$$

being, as has been said, closely related to theine, the alkaloid of tea and coffee, which is a methylated derivative of theobromine. Theobromine is richer in nitrogen than theine, as may be seen on comparing its percentage composition with that of theine.

C_7.	.	.	.	.	.	84	46·67
H_8.	.	.	.	.	.	8	4·44
N_4.	.	.	.	.	.	56	31·11
O_2.	.	.	.	.	.	32	17·78
						180	100·00

Theobromine differs from theine by not forming silk-like crystals, being nearly amorphous. It is, likewise, far less soluble in alcohol. It sublimes between 290° and 295° C.

Its extraction is very similar to the extraction of theine. The cacao is boiled with successive portions of water; the solution is precipitated with neutral acetate of lead, the excess of lead being precipitated with sulphuretted hydrogen, and the filtrate is evaporated down. The thick residue so obtained is boiled with alcohol, and the alcoholic solution filtered boiling. On cooling, the alcoholic solution deposits the theobromine in a coloured form, susceptible of purification in various ways.

Theobromine, like tyrosine, dissolves in ammonia much more freely than in water.

The **cacao seed**, in **its unprepared condition, is not** an article **of retail trade.** Before it **reaches the** consumer it requires much preparation, and without such preparation is in as impracticable a condition as unground grain before the miller has converted it into flour.

Flake Cocoa, which is one of the simplest preparations of the cacao seed, **consists of the seed simply crushed, without separation of the shell (or husk) into the form of flakes.** It is **by no means** a desirable form of **cocoa,** inasmuch as the **husk is** irritating to the intestines, and apt to give rise to a peculiar form of dysentery ; moreover, it requires a **great** deal of cooking in order to render it palatable.

Cocoa-Nibs.—To prepare the nibs, **the cacao** seeds are roasted, crushed **(but not** powdered), **and** then winnowed **from the** husk. **This is a** much better preparation than the *flake,* **inasmuch as it is** free from the husk. The drawback to its **use is, that** it requires a very prolonged boiling in order to become available for food.

Soluble Cocoa.—There are two methods of making soluble cocoa : (1.) By taking the nibs, expressing a portion of the fat, and powdering the residue. (2.) **By adding farina to the nib** containing the whole **of its fat, and** then powdering. (Dunn and Hewett.)

The exact details of the manufacture **are** quoted from Mr **Holm's** lectures to the Society of Arts :—

" **The** mode of manufacture of soluble cocoa or chocolate powder is as follows :—The raw nuts are first picked in order to remove any mouldy **or** damaged nuts, the presence of which would injure the flavour of the cocoa. The picked nuts are then placed

D

in revolving heated cylinders. When sufficiently roasted—a process which takes from three-quarters of an hour to an hour and a half—they are either spread out thinly on a grating, or placed in coolers so constructed as to offer a large conducting surface, and are thus rapidly cooled down. The roasted nuts are then conveyed to a kibbling-mill supplied with fans; the cocoa is here broken down and the shell winnowed from the nib. When this operation is fully effected, the nibs are slightly warmed before being ground.

"A cocoa-mill constructed to reduce the nibs into a fine paste consists of two parts—viz., the feed-mill and the grinding-mill. The object of the feed-mill is merely to regulate the supply of cocoa sent into the grinding-mill. The latter is not unlike a flour-mill, consisting of a horizontal bed, on which revolves a runner. These mills have to be heated, and the cocoa runs from them in a smooth, semi-liquid condition, when it is ready for incorporation with the sugar and farinaceous substances with which it is to be mixed. It is afterwards reduced to a powder. This powder may be made either fine or coarse, it being a question of merely manipulative process, which has no relation to quality. If required very fine, it may have to be more completely pulverised in another mill. But whether coarse in grain or fine matters not; the cocoa is the same in quality—that is, either fine or common preparations may have either appearance. With slight variations of process, this is the only way in which soluble cocoa powder can be produced; that is, it must contain sugar and farina. The cocoa being, in the first place, very finely ground, the sugar causes it to mix readily, while the farinaceous substance holds the particles of cocoa in suspension, and the whole forms an emulsion."

The disadvantage of the soluble cocoa prepared from the nib by simple expression of part of the fat, and then powdering, is, that it requires boiling in order to become available. The merit of the other mode of preparation, with starch and sugar, is, that simple mixing with boiling water is all the preparation required in order to become available for use.

The former of these kinds of soluble cocoa has been rather

unfairly extolled as being pure cocoa ; but it is much dearer than the latter, and is impoverished of a certain portion of fat.

Between these two kinds of soluble cocoa there are very obvious differences in chemical character. The former is necessarily rich in mineral matter, and the latter is comparatively poor.

The following determinations illustrate this fact :—

Percentage of ash.

(1.)	Cocoa powder (by abstraction of part of butter), ...	3·47
(2.)	Soluble cocoa (by mixture with starch and sugar), ...	1·45
(3.)	Dunn & Hewett's commonest cocoa, . .	1·71
(4.)	Chocolate, ...	1·11

A determination of the ratio of fat to ash in the sample of soluble cocoa would obviously afford information.

With regard to the mixed cocoa and to chocolate (which is, in fact, a variety of mixed cocoa), a clue to the proportion of cocoa-nibs in the mixture may be derived from the percentage of ash yielded by the mixture. It is impossible for a larger proportion of nibs to be present in the mixture than is indicated by the ash. In the three mixtures which furnished 1·45, 1·71, and 1·11 per cent. of ash respectively, there cannot possibly be more than 50 per cent. of real cocoa-nib.

Advantage may likewise be taken of the fact that the ash consists to a great extent of soluble phosphates ; and having burnt a sample so as to get the ash, the analyst may boil the ash with water, filter, and precipitate the phosphoric acid in the filtrate by means of ammonia-sulphate of magnesia, and afterwards weigh the ignited pyrophosphate of magnesia.

Inasmuch as the analyst, in dealing with cocoa, will chiefly have to deal with mixed cocoas, I have bestowed some trouble on the devising of ready methods of investigating these mixtures.

One of the simplest and most satisfactory methods of testing these mixtures is by *cold aqueous extraction*, as exemplified in the following experiments.

First of all, I have experimented on the nib itself, as was obviously desirable, in order to be provided with a basis for comparison and calculation.

Ten grammes of crushed nibs were carefully ground up with cold water, which had been measured before being employed, and which measured 200 cubic centimetres. The water was of course added gradually, and after very complete mixture the liquid was filtered. The first portions of filtrate having been thrown away, 50 cubic centimetres of filtrate were then collected and evaporated to dryness in the water bath, and the residue weighed. The residue was then ignited and the resulting ash weighed. The results were as follow : residue = 0·223 grammes ; ash = 0·054 grammes.

Since, however (although 200 c. c. of liquid had been employed to extract the ten grammes of cocoa-nib), only 50 c. c. had been actually evaporated down, it follows that only one quarter of ten grammes of cocoa had been actually made to yield up dry solid extract. The results, therefore, stand thus :—

Cocoa-nib taken,	.	.	2·5	grammes.
Dry extract, .	.	.	0·223	,,
Ash of extract, .	.	.	0·054	,,

Or, in percentage,

Dry extract,	.	.	.	.	8·92
Ash, .	.	.	.	.	2·16

The completeness of this extraction by cold water, in the manner described, may be judged of by the fact of the ash obtained from the extract being quite as large in amount as the soluble part of the ash of the nib itself.

Good cocoa-nibs, therefore, yield up to cold water the following percentages of organic and mineral matter :—

Organic matter, ...	6·76
Mineral matter, ...	2·16

The mineral matter was found to consist, in great part, of soluble phosphate, and it might be useful to weigh the pyrophosphate of magnesia obtainable from it by precipitation with magnesia salts.

On applying the same method of investigation to a mixed cocoa, to Dunn & Hewett's commonest cocoa (which is professedly a mixture containing sugar, starch, and cocoa), price 6d. per lb., I obtained the following results :—

2·5	grammes of this cocoa yielded	
1·151	,,	dry extract,
0·026	,,	ash.

Or, in percentage, 100 grammes cocoa gave

46.04	grammes of dry extract,	
1·04	,,	ash.

If we base the calculation of the percentage of cocoa-nibs on the ash, we arrive at the following results :—

Cocoa-nibs, ...	48
Sugar, ...	42
Starch, ...	10
	100

The object of the analyst in making examinations of mixed cocoa, comprises the question of adulteration with chicory and other analogous matters. And from this point of view the method, by means of cold aqueous extract, is very available.

The solution yielded by unchicoried cocoa to cold water is very pale in colour, whereas chicory (*vide* Part II.) gives a deep colour to water; we may, therefore, avail ourselves of colourimetrical comparison in such investigations.

For this purpose it is desirable to reduce the proportion of water, and to operate on 10 grammes of the cocoa with not more than 100 c. c. of water.

Catechu in cocoa may be recognised by the great astringency of the aqueous solution.

In reference to the different preparations of cocoa, and to the permissible and non-permissible admixtures of cocoa, the following extracts from an Act of Parliament more than fifty years old may be quoted. The Act dates 5th July 1822; and is entitled, "An Act to Regulate the Manufacture and Sale of scorched or roasted Corn, Peas, Beans, or Parsnips, and of Cocoa Paste, Broma, and other Mixtures of Cocoa."

After enacting that persons *not* being dealers in coffee may roast and sell corn, peas, beans, or parsnips, a penalty of £50 for roasting and selling corn under any other name is imposed, and then the Act proceeds :—

"And be it further enacted, That from and after the Tenth Day of *October* One thousand eight hundred and twenty-two, it shall and may be lawful for any Person or Persons duly licensed to deal in Cocoa, who shall first make Entry of his, her, or their Premises, for the Purpose herein-after mentioned, at the nearest Office of Excise, and who shall not be a Scorcher or Roaster of Corn, Peas, Beans, or Parsnips, or a Dealer in or Seller of scorched or roasted Corn, Peas, Beans, or Parsnips, or have in his Possession any such Corn, Peas, Beans, or Parsnips, to make and manufacture in such entered Premises, and with the Knowledge of the proper Officer, Cocoa Paste, Broma, and other Mixtures and Preparations of Cocoa with Sugar and Arrow Root Flour or other farinaceous Powder, such Arrow Root Flour or other farinaceous Powder not being baked, scorched, roasted, or otherwise disguised or altered from its natural State, except by being mixed with Cocoa as aforesaid, and to sell and offer and expose to sale such Cocoa Paste, Broma, or other Mixture or Preparation as aforesaid : Provided always, that every such Person and Persons shall inclose all such Cocoa Paste, Broma, and other such Mixtures and Preparations of Cocoa as aforesaid, as soon as the same is made, and before the same is sold, offered, or exposed for Sale or delivered, in Paper sealed and stamped, or in some Pot or other Vessel to which a Stamp shall be affixed in such Manner as the Commissioners of Excise shall from Time to Time direct for that Purpose, and which Stamp the Commissioners of Excise shall from Time to Time furnish and cause to be delivered to every such Person and Persons as aforesaid, upon his, her, or their Request ; and upon such Person and Persons paying to such Commissioners for such Stamps so to be used Sixpence for every Stamp to be attached to a Pound Weight, and Threepence for every Stamp to be attached to Half a Pound Weight, and Three half-pence for every Stamp to be attached to every Quarter of a Pound Weight of all such Cocoa Paste, Broma, or other Mixtures as herein described ; and if any Person or Persons shall make or manufacture any Cocoa Paste, Broma, or other Mixture or Preparation of Cocoa as afore-said, without first making such Entry as aforesaid, or shall mix with any Cocoa any baked, scorched, or roasted Material whatso-ever, or any Ingredient whatsoever, except as aforesaid, or shall keep, offer for Sale, sell, or deliver any such Preparation of Cocoa, otherwise than in the Manner and inclosed in the Paper or Pot as aforesaid, containing not less than One Quarter of a Pound, or more than One Pound, stamped as aforesaid, or shall use any such Stamp or Paper a Second Time, or imitate or use any Stamp for the Purpose aforesaid which shall not have been issued by or by the Order of the Commissioners of Excise, or shall use any Art or Contrivance by which the Officer surveying such Premises shall be prevented or deceived in taking a true Account of all such compound Cocoa, Broma, or other Mixture of

Cocoa with Sugar and Arrow Root Flour, or other unbaked, unscorched, unroasted, and undisguised farinaceous Powder as aforesaid, or shall obstruct or hinder such Officer in taking such Account, every such Person and Persons in such Cases respectively offending shall for every such Offence severally forfeit and lose the Sum of One Hundred Pounds."

From this it is manifest that mixtures of cocoa with starch and sugar have long been perfectly legitimate, provided no deception as to the strength in cocoa be practised.

Chocolate presents no essential chemical difference from some of the forms of soluble cocoa, but is different physically —viz., being in cake, not in powder. It must of necessity be tolerably rich in fatty matter. It is manufactured from cocoa as follows :—

"The nibs are placed in a heated mill, called a *mélangeur*, formed of a revolving granite table, with two heavy granite runners. When brought to the consistency of a smooth paste, sugar or sugar and farina (as is the case in the cheaper qualities) are added, and the whole well ground and mixed together. When thoroughly incorporated, the mill is cleared, and the partially-prepared chocolate is passed between three horizontal rollers, which thoroughly crush any particles not previously sufficiently ground. This operation is repeated several times, to bring the chocolate into a perfectly smooth condition ; it is then again placed in the *mélangeur* to be finally mixed, when it is ready to be moulded into cakes or fancy forms."

A form of cocoa which appears to be coming into vogue is the mixture of cocoa and condensed milk, which is sold in tins. I am making an examination of the contents of a tin supplied by the English Condensed Milk Company.

In taking leave of the preparations of cocoa, it may be remarked that they constitute food rather than drink, being highly nutritious in every sense of the term. The fat present in cocoa—viz., the cocoa-butter—appears to be of a particularly available description.   It is said never to become rancid, and merits an elaborate examination.   Whether it be owing to peculiarities in the fat of cocoa, or whether it be the theobromine that is particularly efficient, certain it is that cocoa will sometimes nourish when nothing else will, and cocoa is occasionally invaluable to the physician.

PART IV.

MATÉ, OR PARAGUAY TEA.

The beverages described hitherto are in pretty general use in England. Maté, which will next claim our attention, is not taken in England, but is drunk in certain hot countries.

Of the three beverages already treated of, tea is the one which nearest resembles maté; but between tea and maté there is much difference in taste, and though I believe that maté deserves some degree of popularity here, it should by no means be put forward as resembling tea, but as a new drink for the English people.

Paraguay tea consists of the dried leaves of the *Ilex Paraguayensis*, and maté is the name of the beverage made by infusing these leaves. The general aspect of the leaves as occurring in commerce, calls to mind the appearance of senna as seen in the druggist's shop.

The leaves of Paraguay tea are often very much broken down, and mixed up with fragments of the twig.

According to an analysis of my own, Paraguay tea, as imported, contains—

Moisture, ...	6·72
Ash, ...	5·86
Soluble organic matter, ...	25·10
Insoluble organic matter, ...	62·32
	100·00

Of the 5·86 parts of ash, 4·46 parts pass into the infusion, and 1·40 part remains behind, along with the insoluble organic matter.

Being a leaf (and not a seed, like coffee or cocoa), the soluble ash consists mainly of carbonates of the alkalies, and not of phosphates.

By soluble, in the above statement, soluble in hot water is designated, and the 25·10 parts of soluble organic matter represent the organic matter which dissolves in making maté. Like tea or coffee, this infusion contains the alkaloid theine. The proportion of theine in Paraguay tea is said to be much smaller than that in tea and coffee.   Probably this is true ; but in the present unsatisfactory condition of the processes for the estimation of theine, no very high degree of confidence can be placed in the numbers given for the theine in maté. The numbers 0·13 and 0·44 have been given for the percentages of theine in Paraguay tea.

In addition to theine, the aqueous extract of Paraguay tea contains other nitrogenous matter, yielding, when boiled with alkaline permanganate, a far larger quantity of ammonia than could come from the theine which it contains.   As has been mentioned in Part I., Chapter IV., 1000 grammes of Paraguay tea yield to water a solution from which 0·5 grammes of ammonia is obtainable on boiling with alkaline permanganate.

The infusion of Paraguay tea is of a yellowish-brown colour and pleasant taste.   When allowed to become cold it is also by no means an unpleasant drink.   On being kept for some days it is very prone to become mouldy, some, which I kept for some time in my laboratory, having acquired a thick coating of moss.

NOTICE.

For the convenience of persons who may be engaged in making analyses of water, of milk, or of tea, &c., I have arranged with Messrs Townson & Mercer (89 Bishopsgate Street Within) for the supply of suitable apparatus and of standard test-solutions, guaranteed by myself to be correct.

Amongst the many spontaneous testimonials on view at our office, we insert the following :—

October 27, 1871.

DEAR SIR,—Many thanks for your letter. I have myself begun to give a fair trial to Koumiss in a young lady, who is dreadfully phthisical. She has taken Koumiss for sixteen days, and the change it has occasioned has been most remarkable; she has gained flesh, her cough has diminished, and her complexion has become wonderfully clear and bright. I shall put another patient under Koumiss in a day or two,—Yours, &c.,

EDWARD CHARLTON, M.D.,
Senior Physician of the Infirmary of Newcastle-on-Tyne, and Lecturer on Practice of Physic in the College of Medicine; late President of the British Medical Association, &c. &c.

March 10, 1874.

Dr Myrtle, of Harrogate, Yorkshire, writes :—"I gladly bear witness to the value of this article of diet (Koumiss), and look upon it as one of the most important additions which have been made to the physician's repertorium. It is quite as much a true therapeutic agent as a genuine food, and is capable of being successfully employed in cases where the stomach can neither do with food of the ordinary kind or physic."

LONDON, *October* 11, 1872.

Milk has been justly called the typical food, and is eminently fitted for children; but for adults, and all those who not unfrequently cannot take milk, Koumiss is its true representative. The caseine and fat contained in Koumiss are in a state of fine division, and in a very favourable condition for digestion. The presence of the lactic and carbonic acids, and small quantities of alcohol, is, in my opinion, conducive to easy assimilation. The earlier forms of Koumiss form agreeable beverages.

F. ALFRED WANKLYN, M.R.C.S.,
Corresponding Member of the Royal Bavarian Academy of Sciences; Public Analyst for Buckinghamshire, Buckingham, and High Wycombe.

---

9 ARUNDEL TERRACE, BRIGHTON, *November* 13, 1872.

I have been an invalid for the last twelve years, suffering from an affection of the heart, lung, &c. I have consulted some of the first physicians in Europe, and tried the most approved remedies; but I can with the greatest truth state that I have derived more benefit from a pint of the Medium Koumiss at breakfast, lunch, and dinner, than from any other medicine, or diet, that I have previously taken. I have gained ten pounds in weight in

eleven months. My wife and my son are also taking it with great benefit.
I have recommended it to many of my patients with great advantage, &c.

RICHARD DAWSON, M.D., M.R.C.S., and L.R.C.P., Lond.

LONDON, *April* 4, 1871.

Koumiss is a very assimilable nutritious food and potent medicine in close
natural union. I have lived on Koumiss and bread, almost exclusively, for
the last six months, with great comfort and increase of weight, after having
been very much reduced in health and strength. Its genuine worth entitles
it justly, therefore, to the popular favour which it continues to gain in
Europe and Great Britain.

CAMPBELL MORFIT, M.D., F.C.S., &c.

---

10 CHANDOS STREET, CAVENDISH SQUARE, W.,
LONDON, *May* 25, 1874.

A preparation from genuine cow's milk, called "Koumiss," has now for
some time attracted my attention. At first I was sceptical as to the benefits
which were said to result from its consumption, but a somewhat extended
experience has thoroughly convinced me of its great value. In cases where
nutrition fails, when strength and weight are being lost, the virtues of the
Koumiss soon become evident; the appetite improves, and the patient
experiences a considerable increase of constitutional power. In cancerous
destructions and other diseases of the large intestine I have found Koumiss
of eminent utility, and can thoroughly recommend it to my professional
brethren.

WM. ALLINGHAM, F.R.C.S.,
Surgeon to St Mark's Hospital for Fistula and other
diseases of the Rectum, Consulting Surgeon to the
British Orphan Asylum, &c. &c.

---

8 WEYMOUTH STREET, PORTLAND PLACE, W.,
LONDON, *May* 20, 1874.

The various sorts of Koumiss manufactured by the firm of E. Chapman
and Co., London, W., have given great satisfaction to me and others in the
treatment of anæmia, weakness of digestion and assimilation, emaciation,
catarrh of the mucous membranes, in pharyngitis, laryngitis, bronchitis, and
pneumonia, sometimes even at the most critical stages of disease and of
diminished vital power. In chronic syphilis, scrofula, and other constitutional cachectic conditions of the body, but especially in the early stage of
consumption, I rely upon Koumiss as the "first" amongst all remedies used
for their treatment; it improves nutrition, raises strength, and alters the
constitution advantageously.

A. V. JAGIELSKI, M.D.,
Member of the Royal College of Physicians, London, &c. &c.

SPARKLING  BLAND.

MANUFACTURED BY

EDWIN CHAPMAN & CO.,

10 DUKE STREET, PORTLAND PLACE, LONDON, W.

BLAND, the most agreeable and refreshing beverage, is made from milk upon a similar principle as Koumiss, so as to render it a valuable tonic stimulant. By its use the digestive organs are improved. The ginger, which is used chiefly as a flavouring, adds an aromatic and carminative property; but we prepare the Bland also with lemon, orange, and almond flavours. The medical profession recommend its use particularly during inflammatory and febrile diseases. It may also be mixed with wine, spirits, and beer advantageously. The Bland will keep good for an indefinite period.

OUR SCENTED GLYCER-AMYGDALINE CREAM

Is a really useful addition on every Toilet-Table.

During a cold, and in *rheumatic* affections, it may be applied with benefit to the forehead, nose, chest, neck, or any other painful locality.

As a cosmetic it is very efficacious in rendering the skin soft and delicate, and it is quite unequalled for imparting a fresh and healthy colour to the face and lips. For the hands it is best employed at night, and with gloves on during the night.

On the hair, moustache, whiskers, beard, it may be used as a pomade. It keeps them moist, soft, and in good appearance, besides promoting their growth.

WARSAW GLYCERINE SOAP, 6s. per Dozen Cakes, or 6d. per piece.

www.ingramcontent.com/pod-product-compliance
Lightning Source LLC
Chambersburg PA
CBHW030025030726
47499CB00008B/3115